A Note to Parents and Caregivers:

Read-it! Readers are for children who are just starting on the amazing road to reading. These beautiful books support both the acquisition of reading skills and the love of books.

 The PURPLE LEVEL presents basic topics and objects using high frequency words and simple language patterns.

 The RED LEVEL presents familiar topics using common words and repeating sentence patterns.

 The BLUE LEVEL presents new ideas using a larger vocabulary and varied sentence structure.

 The YELLOW LEVEL presents more challenging ideas, a broad vocabulary, and wide variety in sentence structure.

 The GREEN LEVEL presents more complex ideas, an extended vocabulary range, and expanded language structures.

 The ORANGE LEVEL presents a wide range of ideas and concepts using challenging vocabulary and complex language structures.

When sharing a book with your child, read in short stretches, pausing often to talk about the pictures. Have your child turn the pages and point to the pictures and familiar words. And be sure to reread favorite stories or parts of stories.

There is no right or wrong way to share books with children. Find time to read with your child, and pass on the legacy of literacy.

Adria F. Klein, Ph.D.
Professor Emeritus
California State University
San Bernardino, California

Editor: Christianne Jones
Page Production: Brandie Shoemaker
Creative Director: Keith Griffin
Editorial Director: Carol Jones

First American edition published in 2007 by
Picture Window Books
5115 Excelsior Boulevard
Suite 232
Minneapolis, MN 55416
877-845-8392
www.picturewindowbooks.com

Printed in the United States of America.

Library of Congress Cataloging-in-Publication Data
Law, Felicia.
Rumble meets Milly the maid / by Felicia Law ; illustrated by Yoon-Mi Pak.— 1st
American ed.
p. cm. — (Read-it! readers)
Summary: Milly the chicken arrives to be the new maid at Rumble's Cave Hotel, but
when she wants to become a singer, instead, her coworkers must convince her where
her true talents lie.
ISBN-13: 978-1-4048-1341-0 (hardcover)
ISBN-10: 1-4048-1341-1 (hardcover)
[1. Chickens—Fiction. 2. Hotels, motels, etc.—Fiction. 3. Dragons—Fiction.]
I. Pak, Yoon Mi, ill. II. Title. III. Series.

PZ7.L41835Rumm 2007
[E]—dc22   2006003411

Rumble Meets Milly the Maid

by Felicia Law

illustrated by Yoon-Mi Pak

Special thanks to our advisers for their expertise:

Adria F. Klein, Ph.D.
Professor Emeritus, California State University
San Bernardino, California

Susan Kesselring, M.A.
Literacy Educator
Rosemount–Apple Valley–Eagan (Minnesota) School District

PICTURE WINDOW BOOKS
Minneapolis, Minnesota

This is the life of a cool, young dragon named Rumble. When his grandma leaves her run-down cave to him, Rumble sets about making it into a four-star hotel. He doesn't do it all alone. He has help from a picky hotel inspector and an annoying spider named Shelby.

Rumble's hotel is a mess.
He does all the cleaning himself,
and he hates cleaning! Rumble
needs a maid for his hotel.
When Milly answers his
newspaper ad, it seems like
Rumble will finally have a maid.
However, Milly has other ideas—
and they don't include cleaning.

Rumble was cleaning the hotel. He cleaned the bedrooms. He cleaned the hall. He cleaned the dining room. He mopped and polished and brushed.

"This is hard work," he told Shelby Spider, "and I hate cleaning."

"You clean very well," said Shelby.

"We need a maid," said Rumble.

"Maids cost money!" said Shelby.

Rumble put down his brush and his duster. He sat at his desk and wrote an advertisement in his best handwriting.

WANTED

Rumble's Cave Hotel

needs a maid.

Must like mopping and

dusting and brushing.

Must be cheap.

P.S. Must like dragons ...

and spiders.

9

Milly saw the ad in the newspaper.

"Go ahead," said her mother. "You need
a job, and you are good at mopping and
dusting and brushing. Plus, you like dragons
and spiders."

"Milly the Maid. Yes, that has a nice ring
to it," Milly said.

At the same time Milly started her new job, Wilson Wolf came to Rumble's Cave Hotel for a relaxing vacation. Wilson Wolf was very messy, so Milly had lots and lots of cleaning to do.

Wilson liked to watch Milly the Maid mop and dust and brush. They would talk for hours as she cleaned. Wilson Wolf and Milly the Maid became friends.

Wilson Wolf was always nice to Milly.
He told her she was pretty and had a
beautiful singing voice.

"I heard you singing as you hung the wash on the line," Wilson said.

16

"I love to sing," said Milly. "Cluck, cluck, cluck, clucketty, clucketty, cluck."

"Bravo!" growled Wilson Wolf. "You are a wonderful singer. Why are you dusting and sweeping and mopping? You shouldn't be a maid. You should be a star!"

"Mr. Rumble, Wilson Wolf is going to make me a singing star," Milly said.

"Are you sure?" Rumble asked Milly.

"Yes, I am," said Milly. "He says I'm a wonderful singer."

"He's wrong!" said Shelby Spider. "All you do is cluck."

"Well, Wilson likes my clucking," said Milly angrily. "He says I must practice as much as I can. He says I can be a singer instead of a maid. I'll make a lot of money."

"That wolf must be deaf," said Rumble.
"Her clucking is terrible."

"That wolf doesn't know anything about
music," said Shelby Spider.

"But Eli Elephant does," said Rumble.
"Perhaps he can help."

Eli Elephant was the conductor of the hotel's
orchestra. When he waved his baton, the
orchestra played. He knew a lot about
music. He could decide if Milly the Maid
was a good singer.

"OK," said Eli, "we will play music, and Milly the Maid will sing."

"Sing?" said Shelby Spider. "You mean cluck."

"Sing or cluck," said Eli Elephant. "I will decide."

So Eli planned a concert, and Milly the Maid sang. She clucked and clucked and clucked as the orchestra played.

It sounded terrible!

23

Of course, everyone was very kind. They clapped and clapped.

"Encore!" cried Wilson Wolf. "Again!"

"No!" cried Shelby Spider. "Not again!"

"No!" cried Rumble and Chester the Chef.

Even Eli had to agree. Milly the Maid was not a singing star.

"Well, you are right," said Eli. "Milly the Maid can't sing. But she's such a nice girl, and I don't want to hurt her feelings."

So Eli, Rumble, and Shelby put their heads together to think of a solution.

Eli tapped his baton on his stand to get everyone's attention.

"I have decided," he said. "Milly is a very good 'clucker', but she is a BRILLIANT maid. Three cheers for the brilliant maid."

"Am I really a brilliant maid?" asked Milly.

"You are, you are," they all shouted. "It's what you do best!"

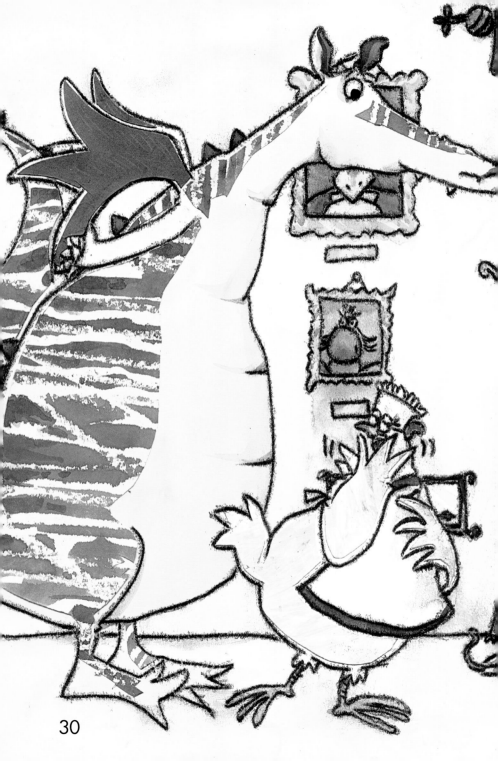

"Then I will be a brilliant maid," said Milly.

"I'm so glad we all agree on that," said Rumble with a sigh of relief.

"But even a maid can sing from time to time," Milly whispered to herself with a smile.

More *Read-it!* Readers

Bright pictures and fun stories help you practice your reading skills. Look for more books at your level.

Happy Birthday, Gus! 1-4048-0957-0

Happy Easter, Gus! 1-4048-0959-7

Happy Halloween, Gus! 1-4048-0960-0

Happy Thanksgiving, Gus! 1-4048-0961-9

Happy Valentine's Day, Gus! 1-4048-0962-7

Matt Goes to Mars 1-4048-1269-5

Merry Christmas, Gus! 1-4048-0958-9

Rumble Meets Buddy Beaver 1-4048-1287-3

Rumble Meets Chester the Chef 1-4048-1335-7

Rumble Meets Eli Elephant 1-4048-1332-2

Rumble Meets Keesha Kangaroo 1-4048-1290-3

Rumble Meets Penny Panther 1-4048-1331-4

Rumble Meets Sylvia and Sally Swan 1-4048-1541-4

Rumble Meets Wally Warthog 1-4048-1289-X

Looking for a specific title or level? A complete list of *Read-it!* Readers is available on our Web site:

www.picturewindowbooks.com